Chime #4
Travelers

Advance praise for *The Mystery at Midnight*

Where's the excitement in a life of constant prayer? Lisa Hendey's latest Chime Travelers story proves that there's plenty of adventure to be had as readers journey with a young St. Clare of Assisi as she risked everything to follow God."
—BARB SZYSZKIEWICZ, OFS, editor and blogger, FranciscanMom.com

"The Chime Travelers books are worth putting on your 'buy for every kid you love' list. These adventures will make you think, teach you both history and faith, and inspire smiles and chuckles. You won't want to put them down!"
—SARAH REINHARD, Catholic blogger, author, *Word by Word*

"After reading *The Secret of the Shamrock* our second-grade class invited Lisa Hendey for an 'author visit.' She kept the students engaged, grew their understanding of the beauty of our Catholic faith, and shared the joy of writing. Now the students can't wait to read the next book in her Chime Travelers series."
—WENDY REVELL, Our Lady of Perpetual Help School, Clovis, California

"Lisa Hendey's Chime Travelers series delivers Catholic values in an entertaining fashion that will delight the young and young at heart. This father of five can't wait for the next volume."
—PETE SOCKS, The Catholic Book Blogger

"Lisa Hendey loves her faith, and that love shines through. Young readers will be entertained without realizing they're also learning a little more what it means to be a Catholic."
—RACHEL BALDUCCI, author, *How Do You Tuck In a Superhero* and cohost, *The Gist*

servant
AN IMPRINT OF
FRANCISCAN MEDIA
Cincinnati, Ohio

The Mystery at Midnight

LISA M. HENDEY

ILLUSTRATED BY JENN BOWER

Note: This work of fiction is inspired by events from the life of St. Clare of Assisi.

Scripture passages have been taken from *New Revised Standard Version Bible,* copyright ©1989 by the Division of Christian Education of the National Council of the Churches of Christ in the U.S.A., and used by permission. All rights reserved.

Cover and book design by Mark Sullivan
All illustrations by Jenn Bower

Library of Congress Control Number:
ISBN 978-1-63253-038-7

Published by Servant,
an imprint of Franciscan Media
28 W. Liberty St.
Cincinnati, OH 45202
www.FranciscanMedia.org

Printed in the United States of America.
Printed on acid-free paper.
16 17 18 19 20 5 4 3 2

▲ Chapter One ▲

"See you after recess," Mr. Birks said over the electronic sound of the St. Anne's lunch bell. At the very same time, the old Angelus bells at the church chimed loudly in the distance.

The teacher's words were lost in the swarm of boys running to grab various balls and head outside. The girls giggled together and reached for their lunch bags. Everyone rushed to the metal lunch tables where the students ate when the weather was warm. Patrick Brady's buddies grouped on one side of the table directly across from Katie, his twin sister, and her friends.

They might have been sitting on opposite sides of the silver table, but both groups had the same thing on their minds: the Brady twins' upcoming birthday party. Since Patrick and Katie's birthday was in the fall, it was one of the earliest parties of the year and always a topic of conversation.

"So if you're getting that new Screen Slayer game," Pedro plotted, "we can all bring our controllers…"

"…And interlock them into your console," Gregory, the class genius, continued. "Then we'll

stay up all night questing in multiplayer mode…"

Across the table, the girls were making plans of their own.

"And we should definitely go over to Fancy Fiona's during the slumber party," said Erin to Katie. "We can get our hair done and our nails painted!"

"Yeah," agreed Maria, "my cousin Elsa had her party at Fancy Fiona's last month. It's the best!"

"You should get Dungeon Disaster before the party," Pedro suggested to Patrick on the boy side of the table. "And Hockey Madness is totally hot, too…"

"I think you'd look perfect in an up-do!" Erin giggled. "Those braids of yours are soooo last year's style."

Katie listened quietly, catching her friend Lily's eye. Neither girl felt ready to spend much time thinking about hairstyles yet. They still preferred horseback riding lessons to makeup and nail polish, but Katie didn't want to disappoint her friends.

"I guess I'd better check out some hairstyle videos after school," she whispered to Lily.

"You're going to need the new Double Disaster controller," Gregory advised Patrick, "if you're ever going to have a chance of leveling up on Hockey Madness!"

Patrick listened to the whirlwind of game names, each with accessories and extra packs, and mentally started writing his new and improved birthday wish list.

Next to him, Peter, the newest member of the group, gave Patrick a good-natured push. "I'll show you some leveling up," the sporty boy joked, "out on the soccer field!"

Both sides of the table continued sharing their separate party ideas. Patrick and Katie looked at each other across the table.

"We need a plan," the Brady twins said simultaneously.

"How we are ever going to get Mom and Dad to agree to this is a total mystery!" Katie laughed.

"We'll figure it out tonight at dinner," Patrick said.

For the past several months, Katie and Patrick had been closer than ever. Between them, they shared a big secret about some amazing adventures that had happened at St. Anne's.

Katie smiled as she remembered Patrick's latest chime traveler adventure. He had gotten to meet St. Francis of Assisi, and even helped him rebuild a church. Katie had not been along for the trip, but that mission had led both twins to help with some very special changes for their church family at St. Anne's.

They were still trying to unlock the secrets that set off their mysterious time-traveling adventures. But for now, they were both focused on planning perfect parties that would make their friends happy.

Later that night, as the twins set the table, they presented their idea of separate themed birthday parties to their parents. Katie wanted a sleepover and a visit to Fancy Fiona's hair salon with her best friends. Patrick suggested an all-night gaming session with lots of candy and pizza for breakfast.

"But you always have the Brady Backyard Bounce Bash," Mom reminded them.

"And your classmates love the bounce house!" said Dad. "It's a Brady family tradition!"

"Daaaadddd!" both twins groaned at once.

"Hoa Hong's even big enough to bounce this year…" Mom said. The twins' younger sister, who'd come all the way from Vietnam, squirmed in her high chair and yelled, "Bounce!"

For the next ten minutes, the Brady kitchen was filled with arguing as the twins tried to persuade their parents. Neither side wanted to compromise on their own ideas for the "perfect party." Mom and Dad could tell the twins were certain about one thing: They were definitely too old for bounce houses.

That, and they both "needed" lots of presents.

▲ Chapter Two ▲

Katie and her friends stood and watched their principal as they waited for the first bell to ring. Sr. Margaret always played Four Square with the kindergartners before school.

"I don't know how she can stand to wear the same thing every day," Maria groaned.

Sister's dark grey habit dress was long and simple. Around her waist, she wore a short belt made of white rope tied with a few knots. Sister wore sandals every day, even when it was cold outside. A plain white veil covered her silver-colored hair. Around her neck, Sr. Margaret always wore a necklace with a small crucifix.

"I heard she's bald under that veil," Maria whispered.

"That's silly," Lily said. "You can see her hair from the front!"

"I bet that veil thing is super itchy," Katie agreed with Maria. Her fingers twisted one of her braids. She felt insecure about how little she knew about hair and fashion compared to Maria and the other girls.

When the bell rang, the friends made their way to their classroom.

"OK, team," Mr. Birks called his students to attention after morning prayer and the Pledge of Allegiance. "Please join me in welcoming Fr. Miguel and Sr. Margaret. They are here to tell us about tomorrow's Vocations Day field trip. Let's give them our full attention."

In their side-by-side desks, Patrick and Katie watched the priest walk toward the front of their

classroom. As he passed Mr. Birks, Fr. Miguel fist-bumped the teacher.

"*Buenos días,* students!" the priest said cheerfully. "Are you excited for our adventure tomorrow?"

The class groaned, but Pedro was the only one brave enough to say what they were all thinking.

"Why, Padre?" he stood and asked. "Why do we have to take such boring field trips?! The new *Dino Danger* movie comes out in 3-D tomorrow! Maybe we could go see that instead…it's science, right?!"

"Now, class," said Sr. Margaret, joining Fr. Miguel in front of the smartboard. "Vocations Day is a St. Anne's tradition! We want you to learn all about the joy of what it's like to live as a priest or a brother or sister."

"Sister's right, kids," Fr. Miguel continued. "It's important to understand what a life of service means. I think you'll be surprised."

Some of the boys rolled their eyes as if they weren't so sure about that.

Fr. Miguel smiled. "The boys will come with Mr. Birks and me. We'll be visiting my friends, the Franciscan friars. Lots of you know Fr. John, who helps with Masses when I'm on vacation. But I want you to meet the other members of his community."

"The girls and I will be visiting my friends, the Poor Clare nuns," said Sr. Margaret. "Wait until you see their beautiful monastery! I think you'll love seeing how they spend their days working and praying."

In his seat next to Katie, Patrick glanced at Gregory and gave a thumbs-up. The boys knew that the Franciscans loved soccer. Fr. Miguel had promised a "boys vs. brothers" match after lunch.

But Katie's mind was filled with clothes and hairstyles and her birthday list. She had so much to do for the party! How would she ever get everything ready in time? *I really need to make a list for the mall!* she thought.

Katie saw Maria roll her eyes at Erin. "What a lame field trip," Maria whispered.

Katie sighed loudly enough for the whole class to hear. "Worst field trip ever!"

▲ Chapter Three ▲

"So, after you pick us up," Katie said to her mom on the way to school early the next morning, "I want you to take me shopping. I need a new outfit for my party. And then we can look at that TuneBuddy I want for my birthday in the electronics store while we're there."

"Electronics store?" Patrick yawned. "I'm in!"

"Kids," Mom said, taking a sip of coffee from her travel mug, "it's early. Let's talk about this plan after school."

Mom was right. It was early. For this field trip, Mr. Birks and his students met at St. Anne's when it was still dark outside so that the boys and Fr. Miguel could get to the friars' place outside of town, and the girls could arrive at the Poor Clare monastery in time for early Mass.

While all the students gathered in the dark parking lot outside St. Anne's to wait for their buses, Patrick turned to Katie. "Try to have fun," he encouraged his twin. Patrick could tell that Katie was more worried about her birthday party than he was about his.

"Oh, yeah," Katie shrugged her shoulders sarcastically. "I'm sure this is going to be just so exciting." She climbed on the bus and took her seat next to Lily.

Before long, Sr. Margaret said, "We're here, girls!" as they pulled up to a very old building.

Maria joked, "It's like a haunted mansion!"

Sr. Margaret rang a simple doorbell and then held a finger up to her lips, reminding the girls to be quiet. "This is a place of prayer," she whispered.

"We're going to spend the whole day praying?" Katie complained.

Sr. Margaret addressed all of them, "Let's open our hearts to whatever happens here today. God is working in this place." And then looking directly at Katie, the principal said quietly, "Consider it an adventure, a mission!"

A few moments later, a young woman came to answer the door. As she welcomed them into the hallway, she introduced herself.

"Welcome to our monastery," she said. "I'm Helen, a postulant here at the monastery. I'm praying about whether God is calling me to become a Poor Clare nun. And this," she pointed to an older sister who walked into the room, "is Sr. Barbara, our extern sister."

"Hello, young ladies," Sr. Barbara said, waving. "Helen and I will be your guides for today."

Helen wore a simple black jumper dress with a white blouse. Most of her hair was covered by

a short black veil. Sr. Barbara's habit was brown and went all the way to the floor. It had a huge white collar that went from her neck almost to her stomach. Around her waist, Sr. Barbara had a white, knotted cord like Sr. Margaret's. But Sr. Barbara's veil was much longer, had a white headband, and didn't show any hair at all.

Does she even have hair? Katie wondered, twirling one of her long red braids.

Helen pointed to a small window covered with metal that looked like bars and said, "Mother Abbess Mary Magdalene has come to welcome you."

"Is she in jail?" Maria joked quietly. Katie shared a smile with her, but no one else laughed. Some of the girls seemed almost frightened to be in such a strange, old building.

"Welcome," the old nun said to the girls. "We're so pleased to have you here today to pray and work with us! As you will learn, we Poor Clares live a life of contemplation here in our cloister. We spend most of our days in quiet work and prayer. But we also have great big thoughts about important ideas—we love to read and study God's Word. We're so happy that you've come to visit today."

Sr. Barbara explained that as an extern sister, she had a different job from Mother Mary Magdalene and the other nuns. "Our sisters," she explained, "spend most of their day in sacred silence."

Katie listened, looking at the old nun behind the metal grill. *Silent all day?* she thought. *Maybe she really is in jail!*

▲ Chapter Four ▲

Sr. Barbara and Helen led the girls to a small chapel where they joined the Poor Clares for morning Mass. The girls sat on one side of the chapel, facing the altar. Behind the altar, there was a wall made of the same metal bars Katie had noticed earlier. Sr. Barbara pointed to the bars, calling them a "grille." Behind the grille, the nuns sang beautifully as Mass began.

Katie knelt down on the hard kneeler, feeling distracted. The room was hot, and she was starving. Sr. Margaret had told the girls they would be eating breakfast with the nuns. She wished breakfast could be before Mass.

Katie's eyes wandered to the crucifix hanging over the altar. She couldn't remember ever having seen a cross like that before. Jesus's body was painted on it, and he was surrounded by lots of other painted saints in the background of the cross. Katie felt like Jesus's eyes and all of the saints were looking down at her. It kind of creeped her out!

When Mass finally ended, Sr. Barbara led them to a room called the "refectory." The girls joined the nuns and stood around a simple wooden table.

"This is breakfast?" Erin asked, looking down at a single hard piece of bread and a slice of cheese.

Katie sighed hungrily as Mother Mary Magdalene led them in prayer. Then Mother read to them as they ate their breakfast. At least the bread smelled and tasted delicious. Katie looked at the wall clock. It was only 8:30!

"We'll never get out of here!" she whispered in frustration.

Next to her, Maria giggled. That caught Sr. Barbara's attention. "I see you're finished, girls," the extern sister said. "Perfect, because it's time for us to work now before we go back to the chapel for midday prayer."

"More prayer?" Erin grumbled. Katie shrugged her shoulders and playfully made a Sign of the Cross, making her friends giggle again.

Sr. Barbara divided the girls up into pairs. She assigned them each to follow a nun for the morning. "You are here," Sr. Margaret reminded them, "to learn from and to be helpful to the sisters."

Some of the girls were assigned to inside jobs like cleaning the refectory, washing dishes, or helping to peel and cut potatoes and fruit for the midday meal. Maria and Erin were assigned to go with Sr. Flor to the sewing room where the sisters made clothes for the poor and for premature babies.

"Maybe we can help get these habits updated to something more fashionable!" Maria whispered to Katie on her way out the door. Sr. Flor smiled, holding her finger up to her lips to remind the girls that the nuns did their morning work in silence.

Katie and Lily were assigned to help Sr. Barbara work outside in the monastery garden.

"Our garden is a gift," Sr. Barbara explained as the girls helped to weed the rows. "We live simply here. We eat only the things we grow or food that's given to us."

Katie and Lily knelt in the dirt of the garden, planting rhubarb and squash seeds. They worked without talking, but Katie could tell by Lily's soft humming that her friend felt happy and at home.

Katie, on the other hand, couldn't seem to settle down. The silence all around her felt so uncomfortable she thought she might scream. She was relieved when Sr. Barbara finally motioned for the girls to follow her back toward the monastery building.

"I am the Caller and Sacristan," Sr. Barbara whispered to Katie and Lily as they entered the old building. "You can help me call the sisters to midday prayer."

She paused in the hallway, pointing at an old bell hanging from the ceiling. Katie could see a long rope attached to the top of the bell. Sr. Barbara took the rope and put it in Katie's hand. She motioned for Katie to pull.

Katie pulled once, noticing how loud the bell's chime sounded in the silence of the monastery.

On her second pull, Katie marveled at the bell's beautiful brass color.

As she pulled the bell's rope for the third time, Katie felt an intense rush of cold wind. The ground around her began to rumble.

And suddenly, everything became a blur.

▲ Chapter Five ▲

The ground around Katie finally stopped rumbling. She realized she was no longer holding on to the rope that rang the bell. Instead, her fingers were twisted lightly around one of her long red braids. The air around her was cold. She was standing outside under the dark sky. Above Katie's head, a full moon provided the only light. Dark shadows fell around her. She wondered what might be lurking behind them.

Looking down the little stone street, Katie noticed old-fashioned buildings and stores. One door nearby said "Bernardone," but the lights were turned off, and the store was closed. Katie tried not to panic.

"Where am I?" she said out loud. "And *when* am I?'

She immediately knew that she must have chime traveled again. This was the second time she had mysteriously moved through time. On her first trip, she'd met St. Kateri Tekakwitha, a lovely Native American woman who taught Katie a lot about faith in God. Patrick had already traveled twice, having visited St. Patrick and, most recently, St. Francis of Assisi. They hadn't experienced a chime travel together, but they had shared their trips with each other the minute they returned home.

Knowing she'd chime traveled again helped Katie feel a little more relaxed. As she walked up the street in search of help, she wondered how she'd gotten here. Neither twin could figure out what triggered the chime traveling. Both were pretty sure it had something to do with bells, since every time they traveled, bells were ringing. But no matter how hard they tried, they hadn't been able to make a chime travel mission happen. They realized that they had no control over when it would happen or where they would go.

And we thought it was only the bells at St. Anne's, Katie thought. But I was at the monastery! Well, I'm not sure what this mission is. But I just hope I can get back in time to plan everything for my birthday party!

Katie wandered along, peeking carefully into windows. Then she noticed an open space at the end of the street. *Maybe somebody will be there who can help me,* she thought.

She wasn't sure what—or who—she was looking for. She felt strangely out of place in her plaid St. Anne's school dress-up uniform and hoodie. Plus, she didn't have her backpack and her favorite stuffed animal, Rosie, with her,

unlike her last trip. She was really on her own this time!

The closer Katie got to the square, the more uncertain she felt. She stopped, crouched against the stone wall of a building, and decided to hide. The darkness made her nervous. *Maybe if I just sit here for a few minutes,* she thought, *I can figure out the mystery of what this mission's all about!*

She closed her eyes tightly, trying to figure out what to do next. Suddenly, something rubbed up against her crossed legs. She jumped and almost screamed, and her eyes flew open. A humongous black cat with tons of grey whiskers stood right in front of her.

"Well, hello there," Katie said quietly, scratching between the cat's ears. The cat purred loudly then circled back and began to rub Katie's legs again. Soon the rubbing became pushing. The cat was trying to tell her something, so Katie stood up.

"What is it?"

The feline looked her in the eyes, then walked a few steps away, up the winding street. Katie watched her go. Then the cat stopped and looked back.

"Do you want me to follow you?"

Its loud meow clearly meant, "Yes!"

▲ Chapter Six ▲

Katie followed her new furry friend through the dark streets. The big black cat ran ahead, and Katie followed carefully, watching for strangers. Before long, Katie began to notice the luxurious fashions in some of the store windows. She stopped, catching her reflection in the glass and imagining herself in those fancy dresses.

Whenever she stopped, the cat stopped too, looking back at her and meowing impatiently. She kept following, not sure where she was going, but trying to trust.

Before long, Katie found herself standing in front of a beautiful home. She waited quietly,

watching the cat meow loudly and wondering if she should knock on the door. Before she could decide, the door opened.

"*Buona sera,* Angelica!" exclaimed a lovely young lady. The big black cat marched inside as if she owned the mansion. Katie stood by the door, wondering what to do next.

"Well, hello!" the young lady said to Katie as soon as she noticed her standing in the dark. "Has Angelica brought me another new friend? Please, you must be cold. Come inside!"

Katie looked closely at the tall girl, trying to decide if it was safe to follow the cat into the wealthy house. Katie guessed that the girl was probably around eighteen years old. Her blonde hair and beautiful dress made her look like a princess. Katie shyly stepped forward.

"*Mi chiamo* Chiara! Please, come inside. You may call me Clare."

Katie entered, saying, "My name is Katie."

Somehow, even though they spoke different languages, the two were able to understand one another perfectly! This must be a chime travelers thing, Katie realized, remembering how Patrick had described his long chats with Francis.

Clare led Katie into a large dining room.

"Another new friend, Chiara?" asked one of the two girls sitting at the table. The girls looked so much alike that Katie knew they must be sisters. The other sister giggled and stood to pull a chair out for Katie.

"Mamma, Papa, this is Katie," Clare said. "May she join us as our guest for dinner?"

"She may, my dear Chiara," said the tall man, standing up. "But, unfortunately, I must leave you. I am off to have a meeting with the father of a young man who might just be your future husband. Please, Signorina Katie, make yourself comfortable."

The man then turned to Clare's mother, kissed

her hand, and left them to enjoy their dinner.

Katie watched Clare's face as her dad went out the door. She didn't know her new friend well, but Katie could tell that Clare was sad the minute her dad had said the words "future husband." *I'll have to ask her about that,* Katie thought.

Over dinner, Katie learned that Clare's mother was named Lady Ortolana and that her father was the wealthy Count Favarone. Clare's younger sisters, Beatrix and Catarina, clearly loved their big sister. They listened to every word she said when she was telling stories. Angelica, the big black cat, was a special member of the Offreduccio family, too!

Katie looked across the table at Clare. Her beautiful blonde hair was shining in the candlelight. Katie noticed a deep green hair ribbon in Clare's mass of curls. *I wish my hair was blonde,* she thought, frowning as she thought about her red braids and freckles.

"Our dear Angelica," Lady Ortolana said with a smile, "is almost as stubborn as Chiara! The two of them insist upon finding ways to feed and comfort the poor."

"Oh, Mamma," Clare smiled, "we are so blessed! Surely we have enough to share!"

"You have been listening to Francesco's Lenten sermons, haven't you?" young Catarina said, laughing.

"Francesco?" Katie asked. *Francis?*

But before she received an answer, Clare picked up a large basket. "Would you like to help me tonight?" she asked Katie.

"Sure! What are you doing?"

"There are many who need our help in town. I'd like to take them food," Clare answered.

"Chiara, can this not wait until morning?" Clare's mother asked.

"Meow!" said Angelica.

Lady Ortolana laughed. "Well, Angelica says

no. Clearly the poor cannot wait for their supper! Be safe, my little light!"

Clare took Katie by the hand, and the two of them followed Angelica back down the winding road away from the big house and into the darkness.

▲ Chapter Seven ▲

The two new friends hurried through the dark streets until they met Lady Bona, a friend of Clare's. After a few whispered words, Bona took the basket from Clare. She agreed to deliver the food to a hungry family with many small children.

"But why don't you take the food yourself?" Katie asked Clare as they turned back toward the mansion.

"My father doesn't want me out in the streets. He wants me home, preparing to be a bride. He even has his brother, my Uncle Monaldo, watching over me whenever I leave the house.

"But it's good that we could deliver this food tonight," Clare continued. "There are so many poor families in Assisi who go to bed hungry."

"Assisi?" Katie whispered excitedly. "Clare, do you know Francis?"

Clare smiled. "Yes! He has taught me so much. How do you know him?"

"I don't. Not really. But my brother met him a while ago." Katie chose her words carefully. It was always tricky to explain where she'd come from on these chime travels, especially since she wasn't sure anyone would believe her. "I came to Assisi on sort of a special mission."

"What is the mission?" Clare asked.

"I guess that's a mystery right now," Katie said with a nervous giggle. "But I know it has something to do with you, and maybe with Francis, too! Can you tell me more about Francis? I heard everyone thought he was crazy…"

For the next few minutes, Clare and Katie stood under the light of a burning street lantern.

"Well, it's been seven years since Francis left his home to live with the poor and to give his life to God. A lot has changed since he first heard Jesus's call. For the last few weeks, he's been at our church preaching the Gospel during the Lenten season," Clare said.

"What's that like?" Katie asked, thinking about how much Patrick had loved Francis. "I heard Francis knows everything about the Bible!"

"His teachings have truly touched my heart, especially when he talks about how we must all live simply and care for each other," Clare said.

Soon, the two arrived back at the mansion. Katie looked at Clare's beautiful dress and remembered the family's fancy furniture and rich food.

"His words have inspired me to do more for those in need."

"But you already do so much to help poor families," Katie said.

"Well, I feel God calling me in a special way to be an even bigger part of the work Francis is doing," Clare sighed. "But I don't think my family could ever understand…especially not Papa. It would be such a gift to follow Francis to Jesus, just like his brothers do."

Clare has everything, Katie thought, *and she thinks giving it all up would be a gift?* Her mind flew again to her birthday wish list and all her plans. She wasn't sure she could share Clare's desire.

"Francis and his brothers live like the poor families do," Clare explained. "They rely on the generosity of others for food and shelter. And they share whatever they have with the poor."

Clare helped Katie settle into one of the Offreduccio's guest rooms for the night, agreeing that she could stay with the family for a few days. Katie wondered as she drifted off to sleep what it must be like to be so beautiful and rich. *And she's willing to give it all away…*

▲ Chapter Eight ▲

Katie woke up the next morning with bright sunlight shining through the window onto her face. When she opened her eyes, she was afraid for just a moment. She'd almost forgotten where she was! Then she looked around the beautiful bedroom and remembered her trip through the darkness with Clare.

"I wonder what will happen today," Katie said excitedly to Angelica. The cat was curled next to her on the soft bed. She meowed loudly in reply.

"Oh, Angelica," Katie laughed. She stretched and scratched the cat's ears. "Let's see what adventure God has planned for us next!"

There was a light knock on the door.

"Come in."

Clare opened the door and smiled. To Katie, it felt like the entire room lit up when Clare entered. "Bona has come to spend the day with us!" Clare said.

As they ate breakfast together, Bona told Katie a story about how Clare received her name.

"Clare is so modest," Bona smiled. "She hates it when I tell this story! But I think it's beautiful."

Clare blushed, but allowed Bona to go on.

"When Lady Ortolana was pregnant, she visited a church to pray for her baby. While she was praying, she heard a voice."

"A voice?" Katie asked. "What did it say?"

"It said, 'You will bear a child who will be a light for the whole world!'" Bona answered. "So, she named her precious daughter Chiara. It means light!"

Clare smiled shyly, sweeping her long blonde hair behind her and pinning the ribbon into her curls.

Katie looked at Clare's hair and that beautiful green ribbon and said, "I wish I had hair like yours! I'm getting ready for my birthday party. All my friends know exactly what they're wearing and how they want to do their hair…and I'm still wearing braids, like a baby!"

Clare looked embarrassed for a moment. "Oh, Katie," she said kindly, "our hair is not what gives us beauty. God created us in his image, to love and serve one another. You are beautiful exactly as you are!"

Clare decided a distraction might be a good idea. She turned to Bona and said, "The Ciccolo family has a new baby, and Mamma Ciccolo needs a new dress as well. And we must get some food prepared to take to old Mr. Antonio. Katie, we truly need your help to accomplish all of this today!"

Bona and Katie giggled, getting caught up in Clare's enthusiasm. Clare spent most of her days in her beautiful home under the watchful eye of her father. Lord Offreduccio insisted she stay home, studying, doing needlework, and, especially, preparing to be a bride. Clare was obedient, but she had made it clear to Katie that she didn't want the same things for her life that her father wanted. Even in her own house, she was always busy praying and finding ways to help others.

"And after that, we must go to church and hear Brother Francis preach!"

Angelica meowed in agreement.

"And discuss your idea with him?" Bona whispered to Clare.

"What idea?" Katie asked.

Clare said nothing in reply, but lowered her eyes and looked out her window toward the church. Katie saw a smile light up her new friend's face. Was Clare planning something secret with Francis?

Katie couldn't help but feel excited at the idea of meeting Francis, too.

Maybe he will remember Patrick, Katie thought. *And maybe I'll figure out the mystery of this mission!*

▲ Chapter Nine ▲

When the nearby church bells began to chime the next morning, Katie's heart skipped a beat. For just a second, she paused to see what would happen. Would she chime travel back home?

"Meow!" said Angelica, wrapping herself around Katie's legs.

"Oh good! I guess not," Katie said as the last chime rang out. She wasn't ready to leave Assisi yet.

Lady Ortolana and Clare came to Katie's room just as the final bell rang. "We thought that you might like to wear one of Catarina's dresses today," Clare's mother said.

She held out a beautiful green gown made of silk. Catarina looked a lot like Clare and followed her big sister almost everywhere she went.

I wonder if Hoa Hong will look at me that way and try to copy me when she gets more grown up, Katie thought. The idea made her smile.

Catarina was a bit taller than Katie, but the dress fit her well and matched Katie's eyes perfectly. After she was dressed, she looked in the mirror, studying the way Lady Bona had styled her long red hair. *I look like a princess.* But for some reason, she felt silly, like she was wearing a costume.

"It doesn't feel like me," she whispered to Angelica. Again, she remembered how all of the girls in her class seemed so into clothes and hair, and how none of that really interested her at all. *Is something wrong with me?* she wondered. *Will I ever care about this stuff the way the other girls do?*

Soon, it was time for Katie and the Offreduccio family to leave for church. Because the family lived in the grand piazza right near the Cathedral of San Rufino, it was a very short walk to Mass. Katie stayed close to Clare. She noticed that her new friend was unusually quiet and thoughtful.

"Is everything OK?" Katie asked as they walked.

Clare looked at Katie with a smile. "Yes," she replied, "but would you please pray for me? I am trying to make a very important decision. I have asked God to send me a sign today about what I am being called to do with my life. I have a dream, but I don't know if it's God's dream for me."

"Sure." Katie gave Clare a hug. "And would you please pray for me, that everything will turn out OK with my birthday?" Katie felt silly even saying it out loud, but she really was worried about making her friends happy. Thankfully, her new friend didn't seem to think the request was silly at all, and promised to pray for her.

When they entered the Cathedral, Lady Ortolana and Count Favarone, their three daughters, and Katie walked silently up the aisle. They stepped into a pew toward the front of the huge church. The Offreduccio name was marked on a golden plaque on the pew. Katie looked around her, admiring the light stone walls and stained-glass windows. The people in the front of the packed church were dressed in fancy clothing. Toward the back, Katie noticed large families who were poorly dressed but still very quiet and reverent.

When Mass began, Katie saw that some things were very similar to St. Anne's, but a lot was different, too! She couldn't understand any of the prayers or readings. Also, the priest faced the altar and the golden tabernacle instead of the congregation, praying in the same direction as the people.

"You are blessed," Beatrix whispered to Katie, "to be able to pray the Mass with Bishop Guido today!"

"Bishop Guido?" Katie asked. She remembered Patrick's story about how the bishop had helped Francis when his father had been so angry at him that he'd wanted to send the young preacher to jail.

"Yes," Beatrix whispered. "Today is Palm Sunday, a special day for the church."

Palm Sunday? Katie loved Palm Sunday at St. Anne's. Fr. Miguel always invited altar servers to stand in the sanctuary at the beginning of Mass and wave large palm branches that Mr. Sipe had cut from trees. The waving palms helped everyone to remember the day that Jesus entered into Jerusalem like a king, greeted by people waving palms to welcome him. In memory of

this, churches gave out blessed palms to everyone who came to Mass.

After Mass, it was time for the palms to be distributed at the cathedral. Bishop Guido stood at the front to give the palms to the faithful. Everyone lined up to kneel at the Communion rail and receive one from him.

But Clare stayed behind, praying silently in the pew. She kept her eyes closed and her face down, trying not to attract attention. When everyone else in the church had received a palm, the people waited in silence for the bishop to speak.

But instead of going back to the altar, Bishop Guido walked to the pew where Clare was praying. As the sun shone through the window onto her golden hair, she opened her eyes to look up at him.

Bishop Guido looked back at Clare with a smile. Then he handed her a beautiful green palm.

"Here," he whispered, "is your sign."

▲ Chapter Ten ▲

As they walked home, Clare took Katie by the hand. A huge smile spread across her face. When they arrived at the house, Angelica leapt into Clare's arms. Clare cuddled the huge black cat and then pulled Katie toward her room.

"My sign from God!" she said as she petted Angelica. "Bishop Guido has given it to me, Katie! Today is the day!"

"A sign for *what*?" Katie asked Clare.

"My father wants me to marry and have a home like this one, filled with riches and servants. But I have made up my mind. I will be a bride… But I want to marry Jesus and be a bride of Christ!"

"Marry Jesus?" Katie asked. It sounded so crazy that she actually began to laugh out loud. Angelica hissed at her.

"Oh, Katie," Clare explained, scratching the cat between her ears, "for the last few years, I have been listening to Brother Francis and watching as he and his brothers rebuilt churches and cared for the poor and the sick. I have listened to Francis preach the Gospel. And my heart burns with love for our Lord!"

Katie remembered Patrick telling her all about how he had helped Francis to repair the church at San Damiano. She nodded at Clare, caught up in her excitement.

"I have been praying about how I could be a

part of Francis's mission. I want to give my life fully to Christ."

"You mean," Katie asked, thinking of the nuns at the monastery, "you want to become a sister?"

"Yes!" Clare said, "but not a regular sister. The sisters at the convent do live a life of prayer. But they take their clothes and their money as a gift to the monastery where they live. I want to leave all of that behind. Brother Francis teaches that God gives us all that we need and that we're called to share everything with the poor. I want to live with nothing, as Francis and his brothers do"

"With nothing?" Katie asked, worried. "But what will you eat? What will you wear?"

"I believe with all my heart," Clare said, "that God will care for me as he has done for Francis and his brothers." She looked sadly at the picture of her mother and sisters on her dresser. "And I hope that my mother and sisters will understand. My mother loves the Lord as much as I do. But my father will never let me go."

"Won't you miss your family?"

"Of course," Clare answered, "with all my heart. But I can't ignore God's call any longer."

"So what are you going to do?"

"Bona and I have been making plans for months. And now, tonight is the night!" Clare whispered. "Tonight, with Bishop Guido's blessing, I will go to Francis and the brothers. I will give my life to Jesus."

"Tonight?" Katie asked, almost beginning to cry. "But what about me?!"

"Oh dear," Clare said, putting her arm around Katie's shoulders to comfort her. "Of course, if you'd like, you may come with me! Or you may stay here with my family. They will find a way to get you home to your parents. I will let you decide. But nothing will stop me from going to follow Francis. And if you come with me, I promise that I'll do my very best to protect you."

Katie looked at Clare, unsure what to do.

Angelica ran across the room, looked up at Katie, and meowed loudly.

"I think I have a sign, too," Katie said, giggling nervously at the furry black cat. "I will come with you!"

"Good!" Clare clapped her hands together. "I have sent a message to Bona. She will come with us to protect us until we are safe with Francis and the brothers. We leave at midnight!"

▲ Chapter Eleven ▲

Midnight? Katie thought. *But how will we ever get out of this huge house without being seen?* There were servants and guards at every corner. What would happen to Clare if her father caught her?

For the rest of the afternoon and evening, they prepared. Every hour, when the clock on the Offreduccio wall chimed, Katie counted down the hours until midnight.

Seven more hours, she thought, *six, five, four... Maybe Clare will change her mind at the last minute.*

Clare dressed in her most beautiful dress for dinner. Then she sat for a long time in front of the mirror, brushing her long hair. Katie noticed her touch it gently once, twisting the end of the blonde locks between her fingers before styling it into a fancy mass of curls and pinning in the green ribbon. *Maybe she'll change her mind,* Katie thought.

Soon, a servant rang the dinner bell, calling the family to their meal. Clare lingered in front of the mirror for just a minute longer. Then, it was time for them to go to the dining room.

During dinner, Katie looked at the silver on the table and the fine food. *What will we eat from now on?* she wondered. But with every hour that passed, she was more sure that she wanted to go with Clare and see what would happen next.

And when Clare's father again brought up the issue of marriage over dinner, Katie saw the reason for Clare's rush. Count Favarone was more determined than ever that Clare must be married, and soon!

"The time for your marriage approaches soon, Chiara," Clare's father said as they ate. "I have found the perfect match."

"But, Papa," Clare said, "I have told you that I am not ready to be married."

"My dear," the count answered impatiently, "this is not your decision. This young man is wealthy, from a good family, and with a bright future. The match has been made."

"But I don't care about wealth or status," Clare said, her voice shaking. "I want to follow God's plan for my life!"

"Enough!" Count Favarone shouted, slamming his hand on the table. "Let us not ruin our dinner with your silly ideas! It has been decided!"

Clare stayed silent, but Katie knew what was going through her friend's mind. She had to go, and tonight was the night!

When dinner was over, Clare and Katie pretended that it was time for them to go to bed. Clare kissed her parents and sisters goodnight.

This might be the last time she ever sees them, Katie thought. Her heart was filled with sadness for Clare. *What would I do if I had to say good-bye to my family forever?*

As they walked down the hall to Clare's room, the clock rang out again. Nine o'clock! *Three more hours to go...*

A few hours later, as the clock on the wall neared midnight, Katie heard a quiet knock at her door. She opened it and found Clare, Bona, and Angelica.

Clare asked quietly, "Are you sure?" When Katie nodded, Clare pulled her into the dark hallway. Katie's knees felt like they might buckle at any moment. It seemed to take forever to sneak down the long hallway.

When Clare passed her sisters' room, she paused and lovingly placed her hand on the door. A single tear dripped down her cheek. Then, Clare wordlessly took Bona and Katie by the hands and led them toward the stairs to the basement.

Every few steps, one of the stairs let out a low creaking sound. "Maybe it's too dangerous," Katie whispered to Bona. Bona's eyes were wide in the darkness, but Clare was determined to keep sneaking forward.

When they reached the basement, Bona lit a candle. They wound their way through dark, damp corridors. As the dim light hit the floors, Katie felt something run across her foot. She started to scream, "A cockroach!" Bona placed a hand over Katie's mouth just in time. Katie jumped around trying to shake the cockroach loose from her shoe. Clare held her finger to her lips, and the three of them tried to keep even their breathing quiet.

But it was too late. Down the hall, they heard the voice of the night watchman yelling, "Who goes there?"

The three girls froze, afraid to take another step.

"Guards!" the watchman yelled. "Raise the alarm!"

"All is lost, Clare!" Bona whispered. "We'll never make it to the servants' entrance now."

Clare pointed with determination to a doorway only a few steps from where they stood. It was covered with cobwebs and rust. A huge spider hung from one of the webs, staring directly at Clare, Katie, and Bona.

"*The Door of the Dead*?" Bona whispered with fear in her eyes. The words made Katie shiver. "Are you crazy? It's used only for funerals! It hasn't been opened in years! And it weighs a ton—we will never get it opened!"

Behind them, the running footsteps grew closer and closer. The bells of the clock began to chime loudly.

It was midnight!

▲ Chapter Twelve ▲

Katie stood staring at the massive door.

The footsteps of the night watchman were so close, she thought she could hear his ragged breathing. Behind him, two other guards joined the chase yelling, "Lady Chiara's room is empty! We have sent for Monaldo! Ring the alarm!"

"Maybe we should try tomorrow night," Katie said, her heart racing.

But Clare turned toward the creepy door, made the Sign of the Cross, then grabbed the knob and turned it. As she did this, she threw the weight of her body against the Door of the Dead.

Somehow, as the last midnight chime tolled, the door opened with a heavy creaking sound.

Angelica slid through the slender crack and into the darkness. Katie, Clare, and Bona followed the cat, squeezing through the narrow opening. Once they were outside, Katie's heart thumped with fear. Immediately, the heavy door slammed behind them. As they ran from the huge house, they heard the guards trying to open the massive door.

"Open the door, you fools!" the watchman yelled.

"We're trying!" the guards answered. They pounded and yelled with frustration as they tried with all their might to reopen it.

It wouldn't budge.

Katie, Clare, and Bona ran across the big piazza in front of the cathedral, then through a series of dark, winding stone streets. Katie moved forward with no idea where she was going. She kept her eyes on Angelica's tail and Clare's swaying blonde hair, praying that they would be safe. She ran as fast as she'd ever run.

As the voices of the guards faded behind them, Katie stopped feeling afraid. She loved the feel of the blustery wind on her face. Her legs were strong as she ran through the olive tree forest that surrounded Assisi. Soon, they saw lights ahead of them.

Clare ran toward the small group of men holding flaming torches and wearing long robes. Finally, she slowed to a stop. Katie, Bona, and Angelica stood behind her.

"Peace and all good!" said one of the men, coming forward to welcome Clare.

"*Grazie!* Thank you." Clare curtseyed before him. "I have come to live as you do, as the Gospel calls us to live."

Then turning to Katie, Clare said, "Katie, this is Brother Francis!"

Katie froze, looking at the dark-haired man in the long robe. Francis of Assisi! He didn't really look like the image in the stained-glass window at St. Anne's, but he somehow still looked exactly like she had pictured him. Especially his eyes, which were full of kindness. He smiled at her and nodded his head in greeting. Katie couldn't wait to ask Francis if he remembered Patrick. She had so many questions for him!

But now wasn't the right time. This was Clare's time. Katie held her questions inside. They followed Francis and his brothers into a small, grey stone chapel.

Katie looked around the dark space.

"We call this the Portiuncula, a little place that was given to us for our work," Francis said.

Then he shared a few quiet words to Clare. Katie watched as Clare's eyes filled with tears. She pulled her hair over her shoulder, holding it in both her hands as she spoke with the priest. He touched her cheek lightly with the back of his fingers, and she finally nodded and turned away

from Francis to face the crucifix. With her back to him, she pulled the green ribbon free, brushed her blonde hair behind her shoulders, and lifted her eyes to the cross. Clare shivered and wiped away the tears on her cheeks.

Francis took a small knife from one of the brothers. He lifted Clare's beautiful blonde hair and began to cut it. Katie gasped. Long blonde strands fell to the floor. Katie felt like she might cry too, but was determined to be strong for her friend. For Clare, there was no turning back. Cutting her hair was a sign that she was giving up her old life to begin a new one.

After all of Clare's long locks had been removed, leaving her hair as short as a boy's, Francis handed her a pile of cloth and a piece of rope. Clare left with Bona and went to a shadowy corner of the chapel. When they returned, Clare no longer wore her beautiful gown. Instead, she had on the rough grey robe with a white knotted belt.

With her short hair and bare feet, she was almost unrecognizable.

The brothers welcomed Clare with smiles and quiet words. After a moment, Francis stepped forward again.

"Your lives are in danger!" Francis said to Clare. "Your father will not rest until he has returned you to Assisi! We must take you away from here. I've made a plan to keep you safe. But we must go now!"

"You lead the way, Brother Francis," Clare said, her voice growing stronger, "and I will follow."

As they turned to leave the chapel, Katie paused. She knelt for a minute and touched the beautiful green silk ribbon that was shining in the middle of the pile of long blonde hair on the floor. "She really did it," Katie whispered to Angelica.

Then she took off running after Francis and Clare.

▲ Chapter Thirteen ▲

Once they were a safe distance from the Portiuncula, Francis gathered the brothers, Clare, Bona, and Katie around him. Angelica prowled around in the darkness, watching for the men who were still chasing after Clare.

"We discussed that this might happen. It is not safe for you to be here. Favarone understands what you have chosen, but he will never accept it. The brothers will take you to the monastery of San Paolo delle Abbadesse. It's several miles from here, but the brothers will walk with you and place you under the protection of the Benedictine Sisters."

Clare was upset by this news. "But I have come to you to live as the brothers do, as one of your followers!"

"Sister Clare," Brother Francis said tenderly, "this is for your own protection and so that the brothers will be safe, too. I will prepare a place for you and send for you when the time is right, according to God's plan."

With that, Clare agreed. "I will be obedient to your will, and to God's will. I will trust."

Katie soon felt that God was asking Clare to trust a lot. After the brothers left Clare and Katie with the Benedictines, the two girls became like servants, spending their days scrubbing and working and their nights huddled together on a single mattress. They followed this new routine for weeks, until Katie was so frustrated she felt like she might explode.

"The sisters make you work so hard!" she exclaimed.

Angelica meowed in agreement. Clare had gone from having riches and servants to having nothing but the clothes on her back. And yet, somehow she seemed to be at peace.

"I am here by God's will," Clare answered. "It is my prayer that I will be reunited with Brother Francis and the others soon. Until then, we must be patient."

One day, one of the brothers came to meet Clare and Katie. He'd been sent by Francis to move them to another location. Katie was as relieved and eager as Clare.

"Will we go to Portiuncula to live with the brothers?" Clare asked him as they left the Benedictines.

"You will have to be patient a while longer, Sister."

Instead, they were taken to Sant'Angelo di Panzo, where they joined another group of sisters living at the base of Mount Subasio. They were very close to Assisi, but it still wasn't safe for them to join the brothers.

"Favarone still has Monaldo on the hunt to whisk you back home as soon as he finds you," the brother told Clare.

Katie sighed with frustration after the brother left. "I don't understand why we can't go now!"

Clare was impatient too, but she understood Francis's plan. "If we were to go to Francis before the time is right," she explained, "I would not only be forced home, but Francis and the brothers could be in danger as well!"

▲ Chapter Fourteen ▲

Not long after they arrived, Clare's younger sister Catarina surprised them by joining them and the other sisters.

"You have inspired me to be obedient to God's call, too, Sister!" Catarina said, hugging Clare tightly. Then her mood shifted. "But Papa is still so angry that you have chosen this way of life. I fear that Uncle Monaldo and his men will never give up until we are both back home in Assisi."

"Oh, Catarina," Clare said, squeezing her sister's hands, "I am so glad you're here. But it is even more dangerous for us now. Papa and Uncle Monaldo will be furious!"

Catarina lifted her chin with a stubbornness that reminded Katie strongly of Clare. "We are under God's protection. Not even our uncle and father can force us from God's path!"

The next day, Uncle Monaldo came with a group of men armed with swords. Chaos broke out as Monaldo and his men broke into the monastery. Catarina stood bravely as her uncle ran straight at her, lifting his sword to hit her.

"You will have to kill me first, Uncle," she said, her voice steady and strong. "I have followed Sister Clare and given my life to God."

Monaldo growled with fury and raised his silver sword high. The sun bounced off its razor-sharp edge.

But just as he was about to bring it down on Catarina's head, his right arm froze and appeared to shrink. The sword fell from his shriveled hand. He stared at his arm in horror and shouted at his men. Two of Monaldo's thugs raced up to Catarina

and grabbed her. The strong men dragged her out of the monastery by her beautiful long hair.

Clare knelt, praying out loud for Catarina's protection. Katie curled her hands into fists, summoning her courage to protect Catarina. She, too, began to pray.

Two men, then three, then four tried to lift Catarina onto the back of a nearby horse. They couldn't lift her from the ground. She bowed her head in prayer as they struggled to force her onto the horse. Slender Catarina seemed to weigh so much that not even all of Monaldo's men working together could lift her!

The men stepped away from Catarina in fear. They could not understand why she suddenly weighed a ton.

"What kind of power is at work here?" they asked, their voices filled with fear. "Monaldo, you can do this yourself if you want to risk God's anger!"

Monaldo, deciding that the men were right, left his sword, held his shriveled arm, and backed away from the monastery and his nieces.

"Let my brother come himself if he is determined to drag back his daughters from this place!" Monaldo shouted.

Clare and Katie ran forward, scooped Catarina up in their arms, and carried her back into the monastery. Angelica stood at the door, hissing as Monaldo and his frightened men rode their horses as fast as they could back to Assisi.

▲ Chapter Fifteen ▲

Francis arrived at Sant'Angelo the next day to take Clare, Catarina, and Katie to the place he had prepared for them.

"Do you wish to be a bride of Christ as Sister Clare is?" Francis asked Catarina.

When Catarina said yes, Francis took her hands in his.

"You have shown great courage in giving your life to the Lord. Your name," he said, "will be Sister Agnes, for you are a holy, precious, and pure lamb of Christ!"

As they walked to stone chapel, Clare said, "This is such a lovely place, Brother Francis, but this is not the Portiuncula. Will we not live with you and the brothers?"

"No, Sister Clare," Brother Francis answered. "We have worked hard to prepare this place to be a new home especially for you and Sister Agnes. I repaired this place with my own hands. Welcome to San Damiano."

"San Damiano will be our home?" Clare asked.

"You will be with us through your prayers for our work and our world," Brother Francis explained. "I know that many sisters will come here in time to live with you. You will be a mother to the other Poor Ladies of San Damiano. You will live simply, in great poverty. But your lives will be rich with prayer. You will be a champion for my brothers and me."

"San Damiano!" Katie said. She turned to ask Francis if he remembered Patrick. But something in the corner of the small church caught Katie's eye.

"Ah, Bernard!" Francis said, stooping to let a small brown mouse nuzzle his fingers. "You have come to welcome Sister Clare and her friends!"

"Bernard?!" Katie squealed. "Bernard the Church Mouse?"

Katie saw Angelica's attention on the little mouse.

Uh-oh! she thought.

The feisty black cat walked slowly toward the church mouse. But instead of eating Bernard for breakfast, Angelica stretched her front legs and lowered her head, like she was bowing. Then Bernard stood on his back legs and waved his tiny front paws, welcoming Angelica.

"Bernard will be your guardian," Francis laughed. "He loves this place as much as I do! And soon, you will welcome many other sisters to this holy place."

Francis prepared to say good-bye to the three girls. The sisters promised that they would be with him in prayer, and he promised to visit them often. As he was leaving, Katie walked with Francis toward the door of San Damiano.

"Brother Francis," she asked, "do you remember a boy named Patrick? I think he met you in Assisi…"

"Of course," smiled Francis, "young Patrick helped me to rebuild this church! When we did that work together, I never imagined that this place would some day become a home for Sister Clare and her Poor Ladies!"

Katie said, "Patrick is my twin brother, and I am trying to get home to him and my family. Can you tell me how Patrick was able to return home from Assisi?"

Francis answered, "Patrick came here to learn a lesson. He returned when his mission was completed. You will do the same, I'm sure."

Katie thanked him and said good-bye.

"Thank you, Brother Francis," Clare said from across the room. As Clare spoke, happiness radiated from her, almost like a bright light. "We

will spend our days here in prayer for you, for your brothers, and for our entire world," Clare said. "We will not live in the world as you do. But through our prayer, we will be a part of every family in the world!"

"I know that you will, Sister Clare!" Francis agreed. "You will live here in peace. Our world greatly needs your prayers and the prayers of all of the sisters who will become a part of our family! Peace and all good to you. I will come soon and often to pray with you and your sisters!"

With that, Francis left them alone in the chapel.

Behind Katie, Clare and Agnes were readying for prayer.

"Sister Agnes, we begin our new way of life today!" Clare said, taking her sister's hands. "Now, through prayer, we will be sisters to the world, not just to each other."

Imagine that, Katie thought as she watched them. Being a part of every family, everywhere in the world! Just with our prayers…. What a gift we can give to people by remembering to lift them up to God with our prayers!

The thought of prayers as a gift reminded Katie of her birthday party. She realized that suddenly she didn't care about Fancy Fiona's or hairstyles or presents. A plan for how to solve the birthday party mystery began to form in her mind. *I can't wait to talk to Patrick about all of this,* she thought.

"Katie," Clare asked, "will you please go to the corner and call us to prayer with the bell? From now on, this is the way that our Poor Sisters will gather together."

Katie smiled and found where a long rope hung from the ceiling. Clare signaled for her to pull on it.

Katie pulled once and heard the sweet chime of a small brass bell.

She pulled the rope a second time, and Clare and Agnes knelt down to pray.

And as she pulled the rope and the bell chimed a third time, Katie felt an intense rush of cold wind blow through the doors of San Damiano.

And suddenly, everything became a blur.

▲ Chapter Sixteen ▲

When the ground finally stopped rumbling, Katie opened her eyes. She was standing in the hallway of the monastery—the one in her own time, not 1212! In her hand, she held the rope to the prayer bell. Her scratchy grey robe was gone, and instead, she was wearing her St. Anne's jumper.

"I'm home!" she said. For just an instant, she felt sad that she hadn't been able to say good-bye to Clare and Agnes.

"Beautiful, Katie!" Sister Barbara said, gently taking the bell rope from Katie's hand. "You're a great caller!"

Katie noticed a thick binder next to the bell near the entrance to the chapel. She walked over to it, peeking at the many pages of writing.

"What's this, Sister?" Katie asked. She was stalling, trying to decide if she should talk to Sr. Barbara about what had just happened. *How could I have chime traveled?* she wondered. I'm not even at St. Anne's!

Sr. Barbara touched the binder lightly. "This is our prayer notebook. We have one here near our public chapel for our visitors to share their prayer intentions. We keep track of all of the people who have asked us to pray for them."

"You really do pray for every family in the world, don't you?" Katie asked.

"Why, of course," Sr. Barbara answered. "You know, we prayed for your family for many years when you were waiting for Hoa Hong to join you. We all rejoiced with you when she came from Vietnam!

"This is our calling, Katie," Sr. Barbara continued. "We are not out in the world the same way you are, or Sr. Margaret is, or Fr. Miguel is. But we're a part of every family. We pray many times each day for everyone, especially the poor and the sick. Our foundress, St. Clare, called us to a beautiful life of prayer and poverty. But we're not poor; in fact, we are very rich in love!"

"But, Sister," Katie asked, "how could you give up everything to come to this place? Was it hard for you to say good-bye to your family and come to the convent forever?"

"Oh, Katie," Sr. Barbara answered, "the things that you think I 'gave up' really aren't anything compared to what I have gained here. Our life is rich and full! And the reason we invite girls like you to come and visit us is so that you can learn some of the beauty of this place, too."

Katie remembered the way Sr. Flor had been so happy to show the girls her sewing room and the tiny baby clothes they made. She remembered the fresh bread they'd eaten in the refectory and the smile on Helen's face when the girls all said how much they loved what she'd baked. The sisters really did seem happy!

Sr. Barbara patted Katie on the shoulder and said, "Come on! Let's join the others in prayer!"

This time, when Katie entered the little chapel, she felt entirely different. She knelt down next to Sr. Barbara. Nearby, Lily's eyes were already closed in prayer. Katie listened to the nuns sing a hymn together, and then a tiny bell rang to signal a time of silence.

Instead of feeling bored as she had that morning, Katie's mind flew to San Damiano. She pictured Sisters Clare and Agnes kneeling on the stone floor of the chapel in prayer. Then she thought of all of the people she knew who had asked for her prayers: Peter's mom, Mrs. Sipe, who was still recovering from being sick; Mrs. Ray, whose husband was having an operation; Fr. Miguel and the boys, who were spending the day with the friars; her baby sister; and even her own parents and grandparents. In her heart, Katie carried each of these intentions to Jesus. In praying for these people, she felt like she was standing with them, giving them a hug.

Before Katie knew it, it was time to stand and join the sisters in prayer. She wished the prayer time could last even longer.

When it was time to head back to St. Anne's, Katie hugged Sr. Barbara and said, "Thank you! I will never forget this day."

"And you, my dear Katie," Sr. Barbara answered, "will be here with us in prayer!"

▲ Chapter Seventeen ▲

The bus doors opened. The girls hurried to meet their male classmates, who had just returned from visiting the friars. Katie ran to Patrick as he was getting off the boys' bus.

"It happened!" she whispered the minute she saw him.

"What?" Patrick asked, only half paying attention. "Let's go find Mom. I'm starving!"

"You know…*it*!" Katie said, as Mrs. Brady and Hoa Hong walked toward them.

"You mean, *it*?!" Patrick said, reading the look in his sister's eyes. "But how? You weren't even at St. Anne's today!"

"Hey, kids," Mom said, "ready to head to the shopping center? Now, Katie, what was it that you wanted to look at? A TuneBuddy? And you probably want new clothes for the party, too, right?"

Katie smiled at her. "Do you think we could just go home? Patrick and I want to take Hoa Hong for a walk. We thought we'd give you a break."

"But...*the electronics store*..." Patrick started to argue. The look on Katie's face made him change his mind.

"Ummm, I mean, yeah, Mom," Patrick said.

"You need a break. Let's get going. Home it is!"

Twenty minutes later, a pleasantly surprised Mrs. Brady was enjoying some quiet time with her rosary on the back porch as the twins put Hoa Hong into her stroller.

"So, tell me about it!" Patrick said as Katie began pushing the stroller down Tree Bark Circle.

"It was Clare!"

"Clare? Like *St. Clare?*" he asked. "I don't really know anything about her."

"Well, you should!" Katie responded. "She was only like the most important follower of St. Francis of Assisi! She founded a religious order for women, and she lived in perfect poverty like Francis."

"Hmmm…that sounds interesting." Patrick rolled his eyes, suddenly wishing he'd brought his soccer ball along. He didn't want to say it to Katie, but he was thinking that it actually sounded like the most boring chime travel mission ever.

"And I was at San Damiano…and Bernard was there and…" Katie continued.

"Wait! San Damiano? The church? And Bernard, *the mouse*?!"

"That's what I was trying to tell you, dummy!" Katie said, not really meaning the insult.

For the rest of the walk, she filled him in on everything that had happened.

"We had to escape through the Door of the Dead at midnight! And Uncle Monaldo was always trying to capture us with his sword! And then Catarina suddenly weighed a ton...and his arm got all shriveled up! And..."

Patrick listened like Katie was telling him the plot of a new superhero movie. He was amazed that Katie's chime travel mission had ended at San Damiano, the little church he had helped Francis repair during his last mission.

"You must have been there just a few years after me!" he marveled.

"Actually," Katie said, "it was 1212."

"Wow!" Patrick gasped. "So, what do you think the mission was all about?"

"I thought that you could help me with that part," Katie said. "I feel like the mission has something to do with our birthdays. Seeing Clare give up everything to become a sister just makes me feel so wrong about asking for a bunch of things I don't really need."

"Yeah, I kinda know what you mean," Patrick said. "It was pretty nice not to be worried about stuff when I was helping Francis build the church. We really didn't have anything but our robes and a bunch of rocks! But we just trusted God to give us exactly what we needed. I kind of miss that…"

"Well," said Katie, "I might have an idea. But it means our birthday will look really different than we were thinking."

Patrick looked intrigued. "OK, let's hear it."

▲ Chapter Eighteen ▲

As soon as they got to school the next morning, Patrick and Katie were surrounded by friends.

"We *need* to talk about your party, Katie!" Maria said. She linked her arm through Katie's and began to walk toward class, telling Katie all about what she planned to wear to Fancy Fiona's.

"Dude," said Gregory, "we need a list of what consoles and controllers we're supposed to bring for your birthday bash!"

Katie and Patrick looked across the parking lot at each other. They'd talked for a long time about their birthday party the night before and had made their decision. When they'd told their parents they wanted to go back to the Brady Backyard Bounce Bash idea, Mom and Dad had been surprised.

"The Bounce Bash?" Mom had asked. "I thought we decided you guys were too old for that…or at least I thought *you* decided that."

"We've been thinking about it…" Katie said.

"…And we want to do something different this year," Patrick finished.

Katie nodded. "Can you go with us to talk to Sr. Margaret tomorrow?"

Mom had agreed to visit the principal with them after school. Katie and Patrick had decided not to tell their friends about the change in plans until everything was finalized with Sr. Margaret. It had seemed like a good idea at the time, but Katie found it hard to bite her tongue as her friends chattered all day about different hairstyles they wanted to try at Fancy Fiona's.

Finally, the school day was over, and Mom met them outside the principal's office.

"I'm still bewildered by your change in plans," Mom said, smiling, "but I'm eager to hear what you want to talk to Sr. Margaret about!"

"What's up with my twins?" Sr. Margaret asked as she opened the door and ushered them inside. "Did you enjoy the Vocations Day field trips?"

"We did!" Patrick said. "Those friars are pretty awesome on the soccer field!"

Sr. Margaret laughed.

"The field trip got us thinking about our birthday," Katie said. "We were thinking that maybe we could use our party to help some other people who might really need stuff more than we need new clothes and toys and games."

Sr. Margaret raised her eyebrows in surprise. "I see!"

Patrick said, "We were wondering if we might do something that could help the Poor Clares, and maybe also some other kids, too."

"Mom," Katie said, turning to Mrs. Brady, "we were thinking that we could have the Brady Backyard Bounce Bash at the Poverello Preschool program. You remember when you told us about how the moms bring their little kids there so that they can go to school or find new jobs?"

Mrs. Brady nodded.

"And, we thought," Katie turned back to Sr. Margaret, "that instead of asking for presents, we could invite people to bring food for the Poor Clares and toys for the preschool."

For a second, Mrs. Brady looked teary. "I think this is a very generous idea, you two."

Sr. Margaret looked at Katie and said with a wink, "It looks like your mission to the Poor Clares might have helped solve this birthday party mystery, Katie."

"Goodness!" said Mrs. Brady brightly, not noticing the surprised look on Katie's face. "It

sounds like we have some planning to do! Are you sure this is what you kids really want for your birthday?"

"Yes!" the twins said at exactly the time. They burst out laughing.

"Well, then, it sounds like the Brady Backyard Bounce Bash will be in a new backyard this year," their mom said. "We'd better get busy planning!"

Katie turned and gave the principal a giant hug. "This is going to be the best birthday ever!"

▲ Chapter Nineteen ▲

The next day at school, Katie and Patrick passed out their invitations. They explained that the Brady Backyard Bounce Bash was back, but that it would be a little different this year.

"Dude, what's this all about?" Pedro asked Patrick.

"Katie," Maria tugged on Katie's sleeve, "are we going to Fancy Fiona's after this, um…bouncy thing? And are you really not going to get any presents?"

Katie turned to the group of kids and said, "We spent a lot of time thinking about this, and we're really excited about our party. Sometimes, it's even more fun to give something away than to get something!" Patrick stood next to her, smiling and nodding.

By lunchtime, all of the students in Mr. Birks's class were buzzing about the birthday party. Some of the girls felt disappointed that they wouldn't be going to Fancy Fiona's. The boys had already been planning for their all-night game-a-thon. Both groups couldn't really understand what had changed the twins' minds, or why they had suddenly come up with such a lame idea for their party.

"Who really wants to go into a bounce house with a bunch of slobbery babies?" Maria whispered to Erin, loudly enough that Katie could hear her.

"I can't believe he's really going to give all of his presents to someone else," Pedro laughed to Gregory, right in front of Patrick.

All of a sudden Peter walked up to the group and said, "I think you guys have it all wrong! This is going to be an awesome party…"

"Yeah!" said Lily. "We get to go shopping for dolls for those little preschoolers…that will be really fun."

"And don't forget," said Mr. Birks, who had come up behind the group, "this is your chance to see Sr. Margaret and Fr. Miguel in a bounce house!"

Soon the twins and all of their friends were giggling at the idea of St. Anne's pastor and principal challenging each other to a bouncing contest. Everyone knew that both of them hated to lose at anything!

Katie smiled at Mr. Birks, Peter, and Lily, grateful that they'd helped the kids understand what the twins were really hoping to celebrate with their birthday party.

"We'll see you bright and early at Poverello Preschool tomorrow morning!" the twins called to their friends on the way out of class that Friday afternoon.

On the way home from school, Mrs. Brady watched the twins huddled in the back of the van in their usual spot, whispering to one another. "Is everything OK?" she asked them.

"Yeah, Mom," Katie said brightly, "but I was just thinking about one more thing for the party…"

"What's that, honey?" Mom asked.

"Could we make one stop at the mall on the way home?" Katie asked. "There's something I'd like to do."

"Are you *sure*, Katie?" Patrick asked, his eyes open wide with surprise at the idea Katie had just shared with him.

"I'm sure!" Katie smiled. "It's going to be great…"

▲ Chapter Twenty ▲

The sun shone brightly the next morning as the Brady van pulled up to the Poverello Preschool. Patrick and Katie walked up to say hello to Sr. Margaret and the other sisters. The twins were dressed in matching jeans and green hoodies. Katie wore her hood pulled over her head to keep her warm against the morning chill.

They saw the friars, who had been invited as special guests, joking with Fr. Miguel. Being around the friars in their long brown robes took Patrick right back to his time with Francis, working side by side on the chapel at San

Damiano. Katie had told him that by the time she met Francis during her chime travel mission, he had had so many brothers with him that she could barely count all of them!

As Katie helped Mrs. Brady tape up a sign reading "Thank you for your gifts and donations," Lily and her grandparents arrived. They brought a red rubber four-square ball for the preschool and a big box of fresh vegetables and fruit for the Poor Clares.

"Best party ever!" Lily said to Katie. Katie hugged her friend tightly.

Before long, all of the other girls in Mr. Birks's class started to arrive. Katie welcomed each of them with a hug. When Maria and Erin came to the table to share their donations, Erin said, "Katie, can we talk to you?"

"We know that we gave you a hard time about the whole Fancy Fiona's thing," Maria said. "We just want to say thank you for organizing this party."

"It's awesome," Erin agreed, "that we all get a chance to thank the Poor Clares and help the kids!"

Maria looked at Katie and smiled, "What's up with the hoodie? Did you want to look like Patrick today or something?"

Katie smiled and decided it was time to share her secret. With all the girls circled around her, she pulled the hood away from her head, revealing her surprise.

The girls gasped in shock. Katie's bright red braids were gone and her hair was almost as short as Patrick's!

"What happened?" Pedro asked as the boys began to crowd around, too.

"My sister's awesome; that's what happened!" Patrick said proudly.

"I donated my hair to Saving Strands," Katie shared. "It was my birthday gift to someone else. They help children who've lost their hair because of medical conditions. So, now one of them will look just like me and Patrick!" She locked arms with her twin, grinning.

"Time to bounce!" Katie yelled, grabbing her little sister. "Let's go, Hoa Hong!"

Soon the twins, Mr. and Mrs. Brady, and Hoa Hong were inside the bounce house for a quick family bounce. After cake and ice cream, the twins presented all of the donated toys to the sisters for the children at the preschool. Then they called Sr. Barbara forward.

Patrick said, "Sister, we collected this food for you and the Poor Clares. Thank you for being a part of our family with your prayers!"

Katie stood, watching her brother. Her hair would grow back, but Katie was sure that the lessons she had learned would stay in her heart. Patrick tugged on her arm, leading her back for one last bounce before the party ended.

As they ran across the bright green grass in the warm sun, Katie decided to take off her hoodie.

Her hand brushed against her pocket, and she felt that it was full of something. She pulled out the contents, then smiled as she looked down into her palm.

A bright green silk ribbon sparkled in Katie's hand.

The bells from St. Anne's chimed the noon Angelus in the background. Behind the bounce house, a big black cat licked her paws and then scurried across the grass, in search of her next mission.

The Real St. Clare of Assisi

St. Clare was born Chiara di Favarone in 1193 as part of a wealthy family. As a little girl, she loved to read her Bible and pray. When she was still young, she learned from the teachings of Brother Francis. At eighteen, she left her home, went to Francis's church, and became a sister. Her sister Agnes and mother eventually joined her. Under Francis's guidance, Clare founded a religious order called the "Poor Ladies." Clare deeply loved the Eucharist and prayer. She devoted herself and her sisters to a life of service, silence, and perfect poverty. Clare lived many years after Brother Francis died. She is the patron saint of television because one day when she was too sick to go to church, she saw a perfect vision of the Mass on her bedroom wall. St. Clare of Assisi dedicated her entire life to the Gospel and died of natural causes in 1253.

A Quote from St. Clare of Assisi

"Go forth in peace, for you have followed the good road. Go forth without fear, for he who created you has made you holy, has always protected you, and loves you as a mother. Blessed be you, my God, for having created me." —St. Clare of Assisi

A Prayer to St. Clare of Assisi

St. Clare, you were a light to many people during your life on earth. You gave yourself fully to service of the poor through your charity and your prayers.

Help me today to give my life and my love to all those in need: the hungry, the sick, the lonely, and those who are hurting in any way. Help me to quiet my heart, to live simply, and to see the precious face of Jesus in the people around me.

May my life be a light to others, that they will know the love of Jesus in their hearts.

Help me to give my gifts more fully to God, who has blessed me so much. Amen.

Discussion Questions

1. The twins decide that they want to do something different for their birthdays to make their friends happy. Have you ever felt pressured by your friends? What did you do?

2. The twins' friends aren't too excited about their field trip for Vocations Day. What is one of your favorite field trips?

3. When Katie first meets the Poor Clares, their life seems sort of boring to her. Have you ever met a sister or brother? What do you know about where they live and what work they do?

4. Clare's pet Angelica is a special part of Katie's mission. Do you have a pet? Why are they a special part of your family?

5. Even when she is living with her parents, Clare goes out of her way to help the poor. What are some things you and your family can do to help those who do not have enough to eat?

6. Clare receives a "sign" at Palm Sunday Mass. How does your church celebrate Palm Sunday?

7. Clare decides to become one of Francis's sisters. What do you think it would be like to be a priest or a sister?

8. Clare agrees to be obedient to Francis and to live in San Damiano instead of with the brothers. Why is it important to be obedient to our parents and teachers?

9. The Poor Clare Sisters are a part of every family through their prayers. Has a friend ever asked you to pray for them? How did this make you feel?

10. Katie decides to donate her hair to children in need and the twins collect birthday gifts to donate to the preschool. What are some creative ways that you and your family or class can serve others to show them God's love?

The Chime Travelers Series

by LISA M. HENDEY

When the bells chime, get ready for adventure!
Join our time-traveling twins for the trip of a lifetime as they find themselves in far-distant lands and make friends with great saints of old. Join the excitement and the fun as they learn a little bit about their faith, and a little bit about themselves.

You'll want to join the twins on every adventure—read the whole series!

Join the excitement!
More adventures are on the way!

Follow the fun at http://info.americancatholic.org/chime-travelers-the-series